SUPERMAN

SUPER HERO!

BY ZACHARY RAU
ILLUSTRATED BY STEVEN E. GORDON

SUPERMAN created by Jerry Siegel and Joe Shuster
WONDER WOMAN created by William Moulton Marston

HARPER FESTIVAL
An Imprint of HarperCollinsPublishers

HarperFestival is an imprint of HarperCollins Publishers.

Superman: The Incredible Shrinking Super Hero!
SUPERMAN, WONDER WOMAN, and all related characters and elements
are trademarks of DC Comics © 2010. All rights reserved.
Printed in China.
No part of this book may be used or reproduced in any manner whatsoever without written permission
except in the case of brief quotations embodied in critical articles and reviews.
For information address HarperCollins Children's Books,
a division of HarperCollins Publishers, 10 East 53rd Street, New York, NY 10022.
www.harpercollinschildrens.com

Library of Congress catalog card number: 2009932796
ISBN 978-0-06-187855-8
Book design by John Sazaklis
11 12 13 14   SCP   10 9 8 7 6 5 4 3
❖

First Edition

SUPERMAN

Sent to Earth from Krypton, Superman was raised as Clark Kent by small-town farmers and taught to value truth and justice. When not flying around to save the world with his super-strength, heat vision, and freezing breath, Clark is a reporter for Metropolis's newspaper, the *Daily Planet*.

WONDER WOMAN

Born on Paradise Island, home of the Amazons, Wonder Woman was given the gifts of great wisdom, strength, beauty, and speed by the ancient Greek gods. Using her invisible jet, magic lasso, and unbreakable silver bracelets, she fights for peace and justice. Wonder Woman leads a double-life as military intelligence expert Diana Prince.

BRAINIAC

From the alien planet of Colu, Brainiac has a brain as powerful as any supercomputer. He travels in his skull-shaped spaceship in his quest to collect shrunken cities and conquer the galaxy.

It's a sunny day in Washington, DC. The president of the United States of America is about to award Superman and Wonder Woman the highest honor he can bestow.

"Ladies and gentlemen," says the president, "we are here today to honor two amazing heroes."

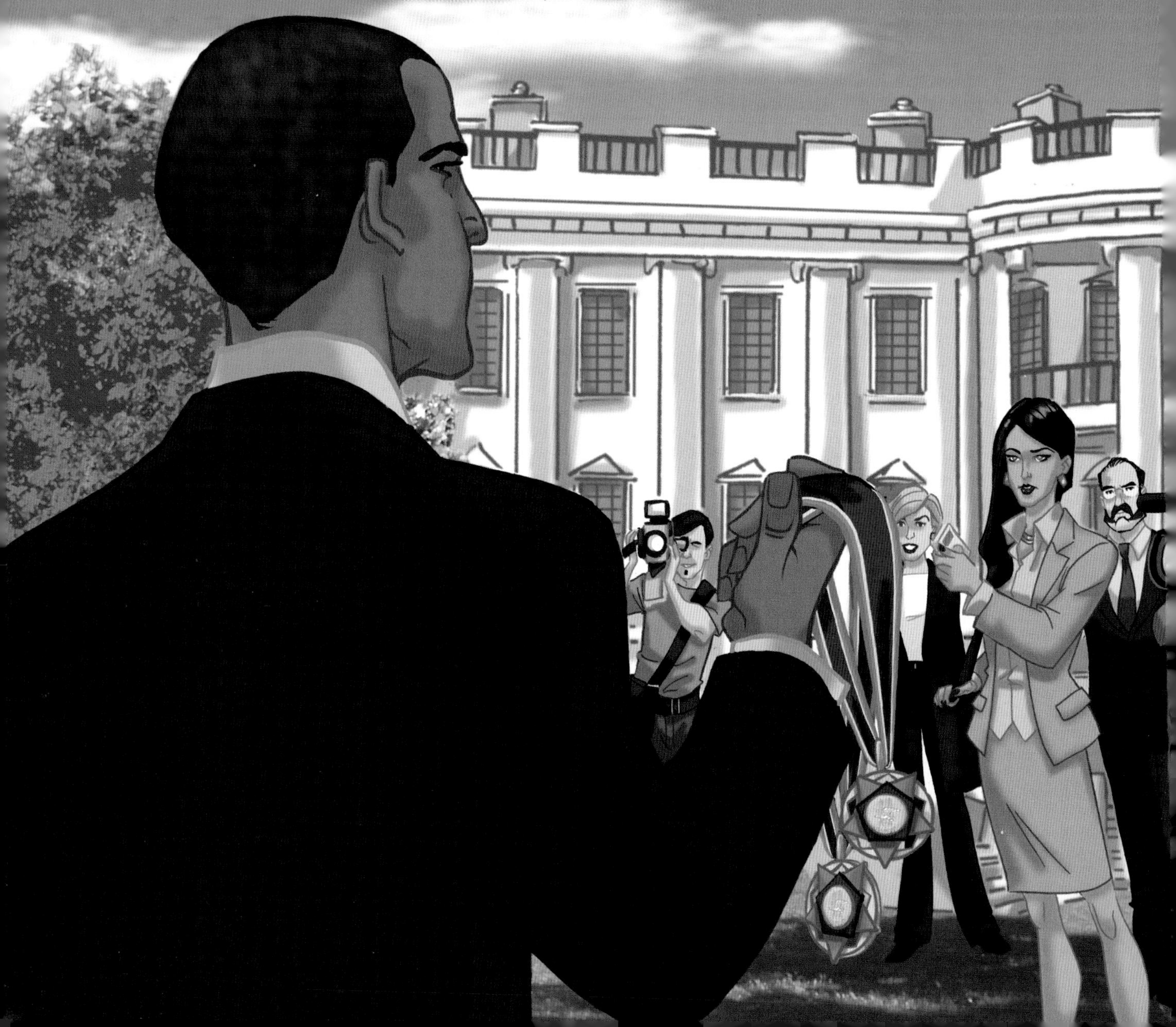

"Superman and Wonder Woman's work for justice, peace, and freedom are unmatched here on Earth, if not in the entire galaxy," he continues. "For your service to the nation and to the world, I present you both with the Congressional Medal of Honor."

Suddenly, Superman sees a familiar sight as a golden glow shimmers before him and an old enemy appears. It's the evil alien Braniac! His mind works like a supercomputer—he is a cunning foe.

"I am offended you didn't invite me to such an important event, Superman," says the villain.

"Brainiac!" shouts Wonder Woman. "Not you again!" She pulls out her lasso and prepares to toss it.

"You shouldn't have come back to Earth," says Superman. He jumps in front of the president to protect him.

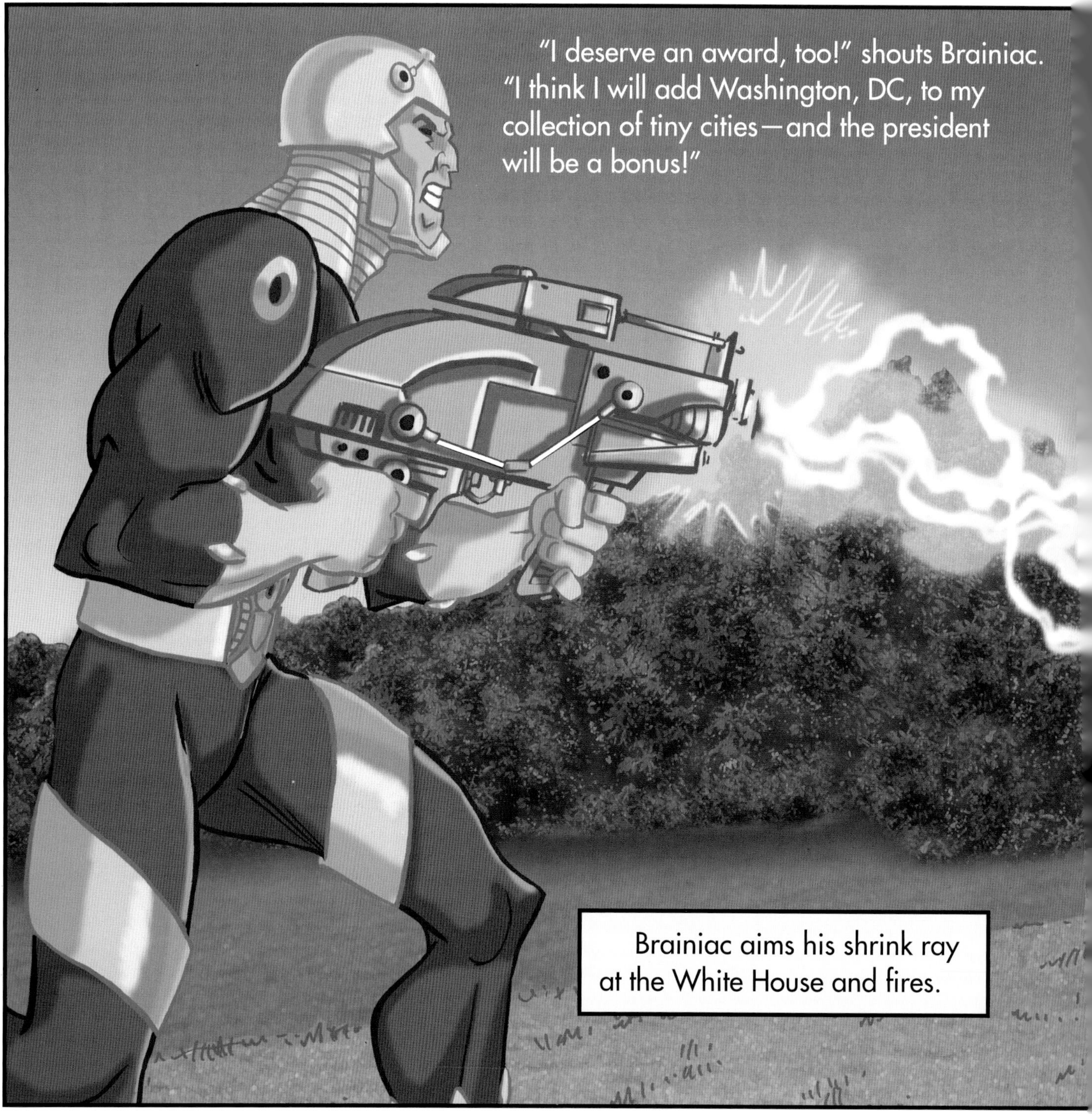

"I deserve an award, too!" shouts Brainiac. "I think I will add Washington, DC, to my collection of tiny cities—and the president will be a bonus!"

Brainiac aims his shrink ray at the White House and fires.

Wonder Woman crosses her silver bracelets to create a protective shield. She closes her eyes as she struggles against the force of the shrink ray and calls out to Superman, "You have to protect the president!"

But when Wonder Woman opens her eyes, she realizes that Superman and the president have been shrunk! As she reaches out to help them, Brainiac hits her with his ray gun.

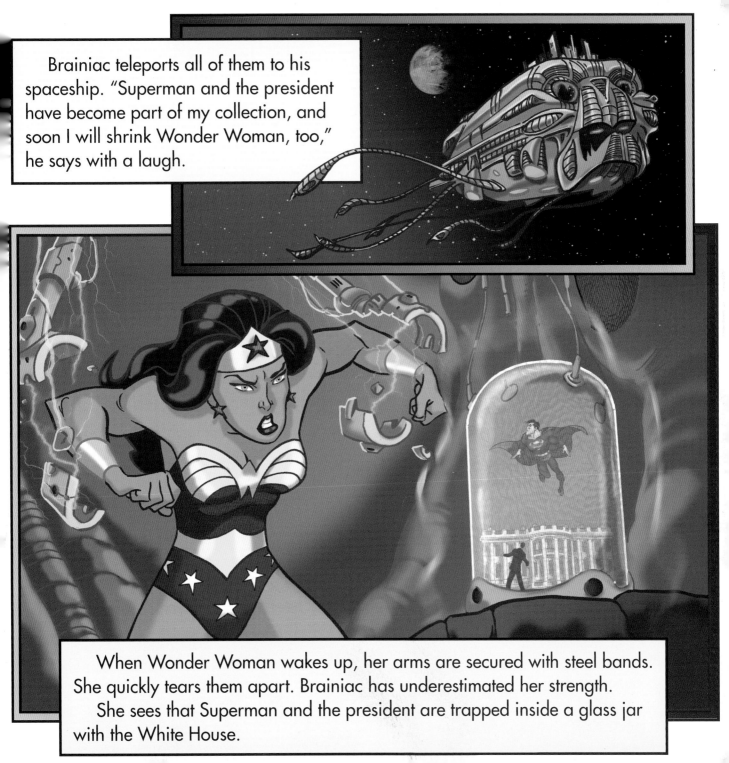

Brainiac teleports all of them to his spaceship. "Superman and the president have become part of my collection, and soon I will shrink Wonder Woman, too," he says with a laugh.

When Wonder Woman wakes up, her arms are secured with steel bands. She quickly tears them apart. Brainiac has underestimated her strength.

She sees that Superman and the president are trapped inside a glass jar with the White House.

Wonder Woman peers into the jar. "Superman, can you hear me?" she asks. She hears a tiny voice reply.

"You have to turn off the force field," yells Superman as he tries to punch the sides of the jar. Wonder Woman finds the right button and disables the force field.

Superman smashes his way out and tells the president to stay put. Then he flies up to Wonder Woman's shoulder.

"Brainiac's force field surrounds this spaceship," he tells her. "We need to destroy his belt buckle to deactivate it and escape."

"I'll worry about him," says Wonder Woman. "You take care of the belt."

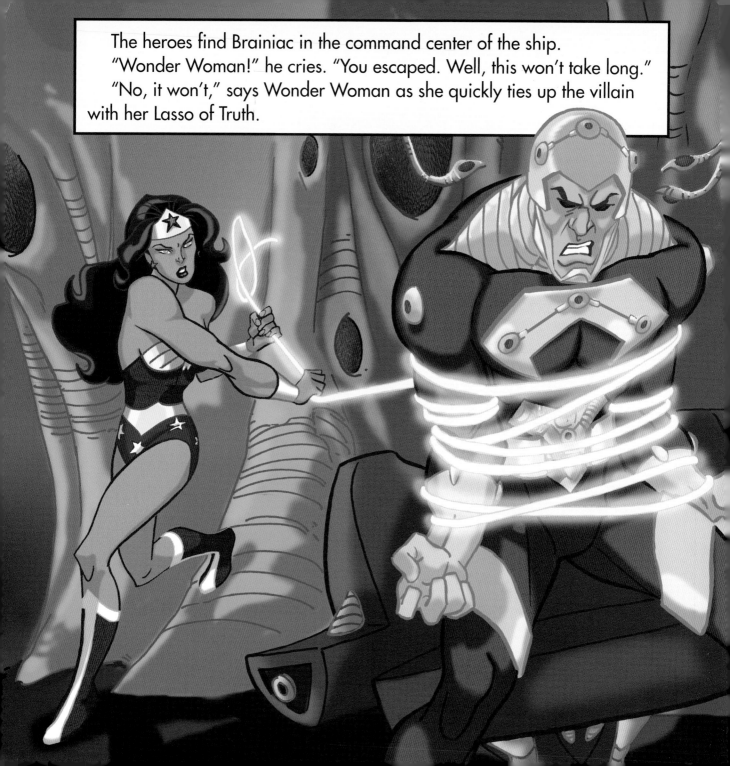

The heroes find Brainiac in the command center of the ship.
"Wonder Woman!" he cries. "You escaped. Well, this won't take long."
"No, it won't," says Wonder Woman as she quickly ties up the villain
with her Lasso of Truth.

Superman flies straight toward Brainiac and crunches the alien's belt buckle with both fists. Brainiac frees himself— but too late! The force field is already shut down!

Brainiac yells in rage. "How dare you, mini-man!"

"It doesn't matter how big I am. I am still Superman!" says the Man of Steel. He attacks Brainiac, knocking the alien off balance. But Brainiac recovers and laughs. "Is that all you can muster, Superman? You will need more than that!"

Then Brainiac hurls Wonder Woman across the room, where she crashes into the ship's controls!

WARNING

DANGER

"Warning! Ship will lose orbit in sixty seconds," blares the ship's computer.

Wonder Woman's fall damaged the ship's control panel. They are going to crash back to Earth if the heroes don't do something!

Wonder Woman springs back into action and hits Brainiac with all her Amazon might, knocking him to the floor.

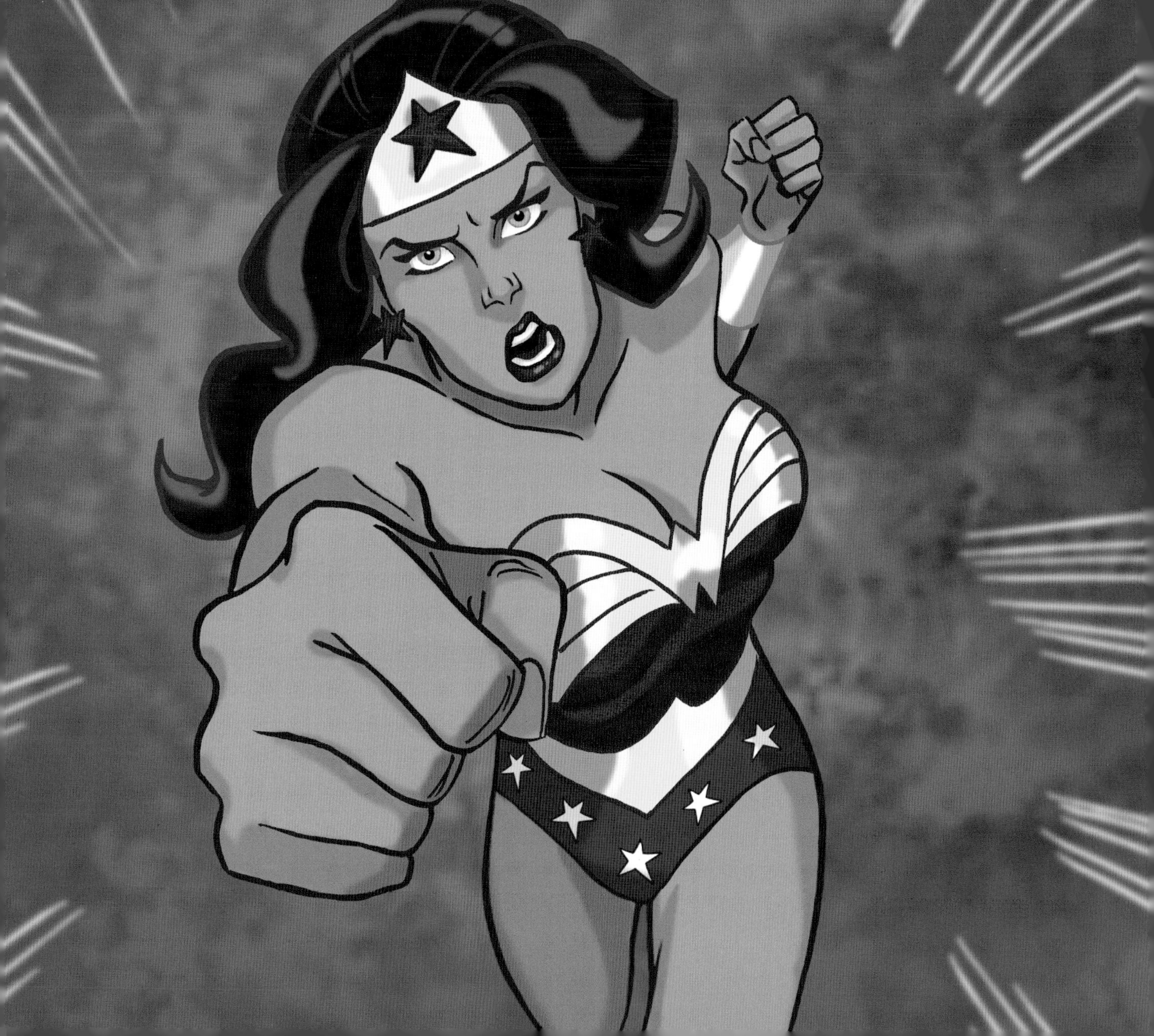

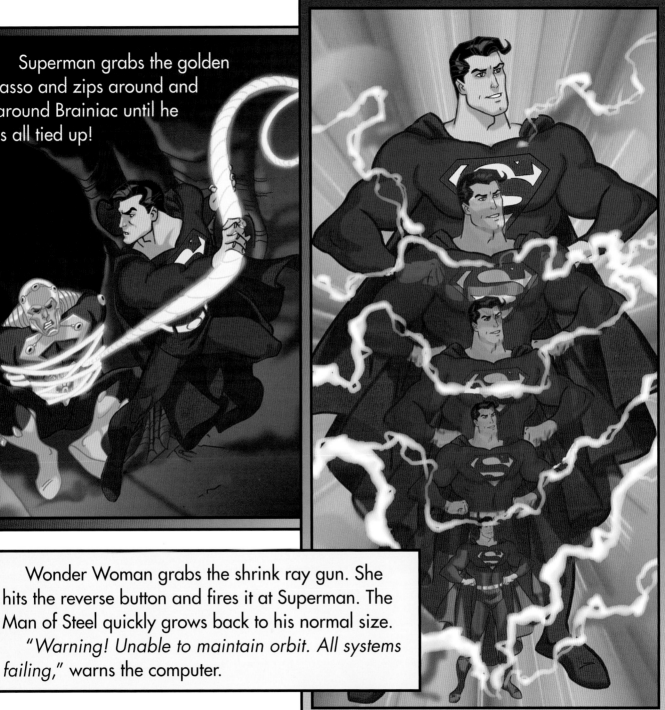

Superman grabs the golden lasso and zips around and around Brainiac until he is all tied up!

Wonder Woman grabs the shrink ray gun. She hits the reverse button and fires it at Superman. The Man of Steel quickly grows back to his normal size.

"*Warning! Unable to maintain orbit. All systems failing,*" warns the computer.

Superman seizes the opportunity to finish the villain for good.
He uses his heat vision to blast Brainiac's supercomputer brain!

"Can't think . . . !" says the alien.
"What have you done to me?!"
"The ship will burn up on reentry!"
says Superman. "I'll try to guide it
from outside."
Wonder Woman nods. "Good Luck!"

The heroes hurtle toward Earth. Superman uses his super-strength to slow down the ship, but will it be enough to keep his friends inside safe?

Superman brings the ship in for a perfect landing. He places it gently on the White House lawn.

There is a loud crash as Wonder Woman rips the spaceship door open. She emerges with the precious cargo in tow. The president and the White House are safe!

Moments later the heroes restore the president and the White House to their original sizes. Two secret service men haul Brainiac away to a special holding cell.

"Superman and Wonder Woman, I believe these belong to you," says the president as he hands over two medals. "Thank you for your bravery!"

"All in a day's work, Mr. President!" says Superman.